To Mimi, my little bat who learned
to go to school on her own.

And thanks to Anaïs Vaugelade,
Jill Davis, Amy Ryan, Marcel,
and Olimpia.

ISBN 978-0-06-307649-5

The artist used gouache, oil, collage, and wax pencils
to create the illustrations for this book.
Typography by Amy Ryan
21 22 23 24 25 RTLO 10 9 8 7 6 5 4 3 2 1
❖
First Edition

Beatrice Alemagna

Never, Not Ever!

HARPER
An Imprint of HarperCollinsPublishers

The day begins at Pascaline's.
Here is her tree house.

And here is Pascaline.

She is five years old with furry wings
and knows exactly what she likes.

Not school. Never, not ever.

Her parents tell her, "The big day is here!"

No. No way. She will not go to school.
Never, not ever. Earthworm agrees.

And all her toys too: No school for Pascaline.

Her parents try to convince her: "You're going just like everyone else," they insist.

"Never, not ever," says Pascaline.

"Go look out the window," says Mom.

Outside, everyone's on their way. The toads, the caterpillars, the squirrels, and the hedgehogs. Each going to their school.

"You're going to learn so many things," her parents insist.
Pascaline grabs on to the furniture.

"And you'll make . . ."
She clenches the curtains.

" . . . lots of friends!"
Pascaline clutches the carpet.

"NO!"

"Never, Not ever!"

Pascaline yells so loudly that her parents shrivel up!

They become as tiny as two peanuts.

"We've shrunk!" they cry with their squeaky voices.

"Yes, you have," says Pascaline, feeling much better.

"Now I don't have to go to school by myself! I'll tuck both of you here, under my wing."

"Oh no! NO WAY!" Mom and Dad yell.

But Pascaline isn't listening.
"Come on, let's go!"
And off they go to school.

At the front entrance, the little bats
are miserable and crying.

Pascaline stands in line
with her parents tucked in tight.

"Come inside," says the teacher.
"Today is going to be a wonderful day."

"First, please tell me your names!"

"F–F–Feeeeelix . . ."
says the first one, whimpering.

"L–L–Luuuucy,"
says a second one, sniffling.

"M–M–Meeeena,"
says another, sobbing.

"B-B-Bruuuuno,"
another says, squirming.

"And you?" asks the teacher.

"Me? Pascaline!"

"What beautiful pink wings you have!"

Her parents start giggling.
"Shh!!" whispers Pascaline.

"Come on, everybody, time
for a song!" the teacher says.

"The wheels on the bus . . ."
sing the little bats.

". . . go round and round!"
squeak the parents.

"Pascaline," scolds the teacher, "stop whistling!"

Pascaline shushes her parents. "Would you two *please* calm down?"

At recess, everyone soars among the butterflies.

It looks like a lot of fun. Pascaline would love to go, but her parents whine: *"We'll get dizzy!"*

"Come, dear," encourages the teacher.

But Pascaline can't do anything with two grumpy parents attached to her.

"What's for lunch?" asks Dad
when it's time to eat.

"I hate pea soup," says Mom. "Will
you order me a salad?"

"This isn't a restaurant, Mom!"

Now Dad is sitting on the edge
of the bowl.

"I would love to taste the pea soup . . ."
And *splash*! In he jumps.

"Now it's everywhere!" groans Pascaline. "You two are really impossible!"

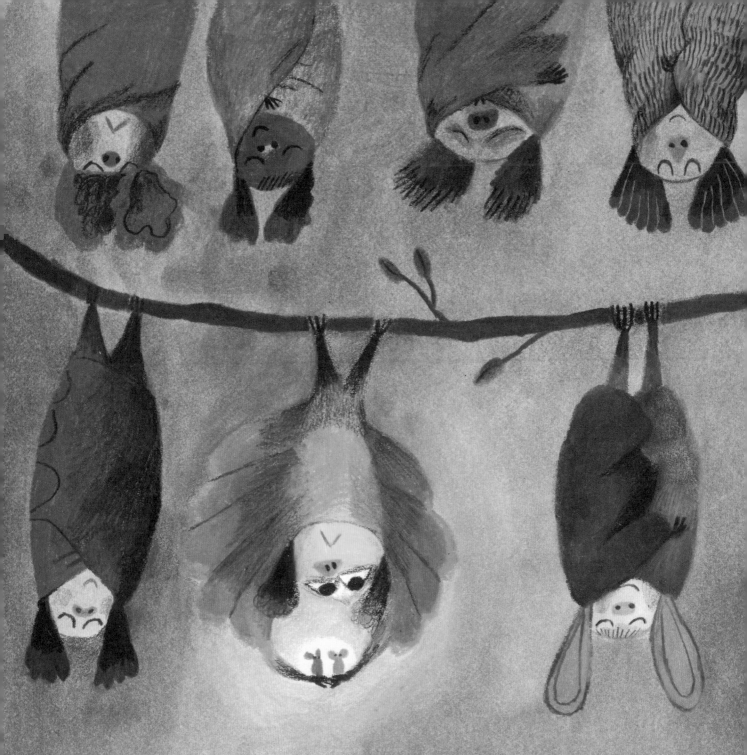

At nap time, everyone is snoozing.

But not Pascaline.

She is cradling Mom and Dad, who are still awake . . . It's crazy. Small as these two peanuts are, they feel as if they weigh a ton.

Finally, school is over. Everyone gets hugs and kisses.

Poor Pascaline. She has nobody to pick her up.

Of course. How can your parents come get you
when they've been stuck to you for . . . five hours?

On their way home at last, Mom and Dad
both take a big, big stretch . . . and, like magic,
they turn back to their normal sizes.

"That first day wasn't so bad," Dad says, feeling pleased.

"We can come back tomorrow," Mom offers. "If you want."

"Umm," Pascaline says with a smile . . .

"Never, not ever."

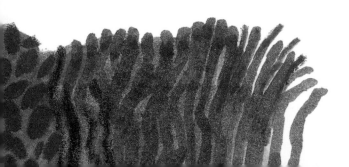